TALES OF THE UNKNOWN

Kenneth Haines
Tales of the Unknown

Published by Spines Publishing Platform
ISBN: 979-8-89691-338-2

TALES OF THE UNKNOWN

KENNETH HAINES

CONTENTS

SANCTION

DIVINE ENTITIES

SANCTION

CHAPTER ONE
FOREST WIZARD

IN THE VALLEY far away from humans lies a dense forest, Always covered with an eerie mist, and storms will always begin from within and become major storms across the region. This forest is banned for any humans, word has it only one person living or dead resigns in this forest and he is called Sanction, He oversees the forest and its creatures. They say the trees and foliage are alive and when humans enter they are never seen or heard from again.

Word in the forest was that something wasn't right and the creatures were on edge and the slightest noise or movement made them run for cover. Word of this came to Sanction while he was foliage for food. The ground was moving towards him and a vine pointed towards the west, Sanction gathered up his staff and cloak and headed into the forest mist and in doing so he disappeared into a thousands of red and black moths flying towards the west.

Meanwhile on the west side of the forest a wagon rolled up and tossed a young girl child from it, she was wrapped inside a burlap potato bag and was tossed aside like trash. As she hit the ground and started rolling down towards the sharp briers that were covering the ground against the forbidden forest. The briers ripping threw the burlap bag slicing her as she tumbles past them into the forest floor.

The forest mist roused enough to illuminate the forest ground foliage, she was able to break free of her bondage and crawled against a large tree. Here she cuddles into a ball and lays down on the ground, tears flowing from her eyes and settling into the dirt below her. The forest sensed her grieving and the vines wanted so badly to comfort her but knew it was not the right thing to do yet.

Blood is trickling down her legs and arms from all the brier slices she encountered going through the briers and realizing there's no turning back. She looks at her hands and arms and seeing not only the dripping cuts of blood she sees her skin becoming more green than once seen. She doesn't understand what is happening to her or why the colony banishes her. She crumbles back onto the ground crying for mercy.

The creatures of this forbidden forest stay hidden and only watching her, all you can see in the mist that surrounds the clear area is different size red eyes. The foliage moved aside so as not to disturb her, for fear of how she would act and didn't want her running back into the sharp briers. She hears rustling in the bushes covered by the mist and she sits up and against the big tree base and wraps her arms around her folded up legs, she can see some red eyes and tries not to look at them.

Fear is building inside her and she is shivering also, Is this the end for her, is the tales of what villagers said about this forest true," no human who enters ever are heard from or seen again" She hears whispers something she never heard before. She sees the area filling up with red and black moths and a hissing sound that surrounds her, she looking around and sees just the moths and can now hear their wings flapping in the air it's getting louder and more are coming.

As the moths envelop her, she feels a mixture of fear and awe. The forest's creatures watch silently, their eyes gleaming in the mist. The girl feels a strange connection to the moths, sensing the presence of something drawing near. The moths coalesce into his form, revealing the forest wizard in all his enigmatic glory.

CHAPTER TWO
SANCTION APPEARS

THE MOTHS COALESCE into a form of a dark figure, A figure wearing a black cloak and a worn old pointy hat with wide brim, holding onto a weird shaped staff, only thing she can see is the whites of his eyes underneath the dark brim of his hat. The foliage raised up around his legs, Vines underneath his arms to steady him as the last moth faded into his body. The foliage released him and he knelt down in front of the young girl. In a low strong sensitive voice he asked why she was crying and why she was here in this forbidden forest.

At first seeing the moths forming a body she was afraid but knew there was no place to run to or hide she had to be at whatever this was mercy and prayed it wasn't the last thing she was going to see, seeing things of the stories villagers told flashed in her mind, Is death going to follow her, she never going to find answers why she turning green?

When she heard his voice it cut through her fear like a beacon. A sense of calm despite her terror. He assures her no harm will come to her. But rather a new beginning. She explains how she was treated by her villagers and was thrown into a potato sack and tossed aside like trash, all because she was showing signs of changing? Sign to which she doesn't understand. Why am I turning green? She asked him....

He slowly reached his hand towards her and she slowly held on to it feeling the warmth in his hand against hers. He sat down in front of her and slowly lifted off his worn old hat and she saw the face of a worn old man. Child please dry them tears for you are safe in my forest, like I said no harm will come to you. She sits up and listens to his every word.

The bushes rustled and parted and a big monstrous hairy creature leapt out from the mist and attacked the old man, but the old man didn't budge from his spot and just let this big enormous creature wrapped its big paws around his neck. She screams out as it attacks him but seeing him not moving or fighting it was unnerving to her.

She watches the big creature starting to lick the old mans face and the old man let go of her hand and gave this big creature a good hug. There is no fear young one this here is my forest protector. Well he really protects this forest and its creatures within. I named him Thor from the strong gods above and (whispers to her, He really a pussy cat but don't let him know that).

Thor was an enormous black hairy wolf, His eyes were bright red and his teeth bright yellow. Both stood out once he is in the mist. It let loose of the old man and towered over the young girl, she felt the fear as it sniffed her and nudge her this way and that way. It sucked in a deep breath of her scent and raised its head showed her his yellow teeth and she sees the saliva dripping from his fangs then he raised his head higher into the air and let out a deafening howl.

He then lays down beside her and I knotted okay and she started rubbing his massive back. She watches the foliage moving behind him and just watched and the vines tapped him on the shoulder and another pointed to her.

Yes I see as he looks at her and she is looking at him, she has a sense of her surroundings, she feeling things she never felt before, she feels connected to the forest but doesn't understand any of what is happening.

He takes her hand again and starts to explain to her what is happening to her, How the forest magic has recognized her and that she's becoming an integral part of its fabric and she was chosen when she was born.

CHAPTER THREE
THE CHOSEN ONE

SHE DOESN'T UNDERSTAND how she could be the chosen one, how and why her?? The skies darken, The massive wolf got up and looked up at the dark clouds forming. The old man stood up and put on his worn hat and motioned the young girl to him and grabbed his weird staff, As she got against him he through over her his cloak and all the red and black moths started to take his black figure and they disassembled them both and flew towards the south of the forest.

With the hissing noise she heard inside his cloak was getting louder and louder, He opened his cloak and she saw the moths coming into his back from the dark forest, As the last one disappeared behind him he again spoke to her, "follow me child." She looks around and sees she is no longer in the same area as she entered the forest and she hears in the distance the massive wolf howling.

There among her was ancient stone ruins stood before us, partially hidden by vines and foliage, The structures were unlike anything I had ever seen—tall and imposing, yet covered in vibrant flora, The air was thick with the scent of blooming flowers, their colors vibrant against the green foliage.

The mist is no longer visible or the threatening storm that was forming. She watches the foliage moving against the ruins and across the ground, clearing a path for them to follow. They arrived at a very large tree and she sees it is a living tree but it's hollow and a dim light is burning inside and sees steps leading up to a doorway. She follows him and looking every which way taking in her surroundings. Once inside He disrobes his cloak and old worn hat and hung them on a hook by the door. "Come in child, make yourself comfortable." She watches him fill a small hanging pot with water and as he sets it hanging what looks like a fireplace flames lit up underneath it.

As the flames flicker underneath the hanging pot, casting a soft glow inside the hollow tree, he turns to her with a gentle smile. I am Sanction, the guardian of the forest and its habitats, he said in a calm, resonant voice."This place and all within it, are under my care, and Thor who you met earlier protects the grounds surrounding this forbidden forest.

She feels a strange sense of comfort in his presence. She takes a deep breath and meets his gaze."My name Liorael" she says her voice trembling slightly."I don't understand why I'm here or why I'm I turning green, or why was I cast from my family, Like I didn't matter?(Tears began to run down her cheeks) She just realizing what happens to people who venture into this forbidden forest and Thor finds them. She feels a shiver running up her spine, just thinking about it.

Sanction nods thoughtfully. "Liorael, the forest has chosen you for a reason. You have a unique connection to its magic, and it will reveal itself to you in time. For now, rest and gather your strength. There is much to learn and many adventures ahead."

Liorael feels a mix of relief and curiosity as she begins to accept her new reality. The ancient stone ruins, the living tree, and the guardian himself all seem to pulse with a magic that she is only beginning to understand.

Sanction listens to Liorael's trembling voice, his heart aching for her pain. He gently places a hand on her shoulder, offering comfort.

"Liorael, you matter more than you know. The forest sees something special in you, something your family and village couldn't understand. Your transformation is a sign of your unique connection to this place."

During our discussion the massive Wolf walks in and lays down in front of the fireplace, Liorael seeing him, goes over and sits beside him, rubbing his thick fur on his back.

Thor, the massive black wolf, lays protectively nearby, his red eyes gleaming with understanding. Sanction's calm presence and Thor's silent vigilance create a sense of safety amidst the unknown.

"The forest's magic is ancient and powerful," Sanction continues. "It chose you because you have the strength to embrace it and the heart to protect it. Your journey won't be easy, but you won't be alone. I will guide you, and Thor will watch over you."

Liorael, tears still streaming down her cheeks, begins to feel a glimmer of hope. She realizes that her past does not define her, and her future holds the promise of something extraordinary.

Sanction offered her a cup of sweet barley tea, from the water he was boiling, She drank hers beside Thor and Sanction sat just outside on the steps giving her some thinking space. Liorael sips the sweet barley tea, the warmth of the cup soothing her as she sits beside Thor, gently stroking his thick fur. The fire crackles softly, its glow casting comforting shadows around the hollow tree. Outside, Sanction sits on the steps, giving her the space she needs to process her thoughts.

She glances at the ancient stone ruins visible through the doorway, the vibrant flora and intricate structures hinting at secrets yet to be uncovered. Liorael's mind races with questions, but for now, she finds solace in the simple act of sitting quietly, feeling the gentle rise and fall of Thor's breath beside her.

The connection she feels to Sanction, Thor, and the forest starts to solidify, a small ember of hope igniting within her. She knows that her journey is just beginning, and while it is fraught with unknowns, she feels a growing sense of purpose. Sanction looks in on Liorael, seeing her slumbering peacefully against Thor's massive form. A soft smile crosses his weathered face as he quietly retrieves a blanket. He drapes it gently over her, his voice a soothing whisper, "Sleep, child. There is so much you must learn before the time arrives."

The fire crackles softly, casting a warm glow around the room. The ancient ruins outside stand as silent guardians, their secrets waiting to be unveiled. Liorael's breathing steadies, and for a moment, all is calm in the enchanted forest.

Sanction settled into his old, worn-out chair, the weight of the world resting on his shoulders. As he drifted off to sleep, his thoughts were consumed by the secret he had been guarding—the real reason Liorael was chosen. He knew his time as the forest's guardian was drawing to an end, and the responsibility of passing on the mantle weighed heavily on him.

In the quiet of the hollow tree, with the fire casting gentle shadows, Sanction's mind raced with memories and visions of the forest's past and future. How would he explain to Liorael the ancient prophecy that foretold her arrival? How could he prepare her for the immense challenges and responsibilities that awaited her?

Liorael, the child of the forest's magic, was destined to become its new protector. But the path ahead was fraught with danger and uncertainty. Sanction's heart ached with the knowledge that he had to guide her, yet also prepare to let go.

As the fire crackled softly and Thor watched over them, Sanction's resolve strengthened. He would find the right moment to share the truth with Liorael, and he would ensure that she understood her role in the grand tapestry of the forest's destiny.

For now, he allowed himself a brief respite, knowing that tomorrow would bring new challenges and revelations.

CHAPTER FOUR
HER TRANSFORMATION

AS THE DAYS PASSED, Liorael's transformation became more pronounced. Her skin, once a soft human hue, now bore a vibrant green tint that glistened in the dappled sunlight. Her senses sharpened, allowing her to perceive the whispers of the forest with newfound clarity. What once seemed like random rustling or distant murmurs now took form as the voices of the forest's creatures and the foliage itself, sharing their secrets and wisdom.

Sanction, with his ancient knowledge and patience, guided her through each step of this metamorphosis. He taught her how to listen to the forest, to understand its language, and to harness the magic that flowed through her veins. Skills that would have taken a lifetime to master came to her with an almost intuitive ease under his guidance.

Liorael learned to communicate with the creatures, forming bonds that were as strong as they were mysterious. She could sense their emotions, understand their needs, and even guide them with a mere thought. The forest became her home, and its inhabitants her family.

Sanction watched her growth with a mix of pride and sorrow, knowing that his time was nearing its end, but also recognizing the strength and potential within Liorael. She was becoming everything the forest needed her to be, and more.

Liorael noticed something was off with her skin color and didn't understand what was happening. It started to change color as she was close to something other than it being green. She ran to Sanction for answers. Sanction heard her running towards their habitat and sees how much she has transformed. Her body had become sleek and muscular, her movements fluid and silent.

Liorael burst into their habitat, breathless and visibly distressed. "Sanction, something's wrong," she panted, her voice tinged with fear and confusion. "My skin, it's changing color. It's not just green anymore. What's happening to me?" He approached her calmly, taking in the sight of her changing skin.

"Liorael," he said gently, "this is part of your transformation. The forest's magic is merging with you, adapting you to become one with it. Your skin changing color means you're gaining new abilities. It's a sign of your deepening connection and your growing power." "Your transformation is giving you the ability to be a chameleon," Sanction continued, his voice calm and reassuring. "This will allow you to hide if danger arises, blending seamlessly with your surroundings. It's a crucial skill for a guardian of the forest."

He reached out, placing a reassuring hand on her shoulder. "Each color will help you blend in with different surroundings, making you a true guardian of the forest. It's a gift, not something to fear." Liorael looked down at her hands, watching the shifting colors with a mix of awe and uncertainty. "I don't understand all of this," she admitted, her voice softer now. "But I trust you."

Sanction smiled, his eyes filled with warmth. "And I trust you, Liorael. Together, we'll uncover all the secrets of the forest's magic. You're becoming who you were always meant to be." Liorael looked at her hands once more, watching the colors shift and change. The fear that had gripped her started to ease, replaced by a sense of awe and wonder at the forest's magic.

"I'll guide you on how to harness this power," Sanction said. "It's part of the forest's protection, a gift that will help you navigate the dangers and mysteries that lie ahead." Liorael nodded, determination in her eyes. "I understand now. I'll use this gift to protect the forest and its creatures."

Sanction smiled, proud of her growing strength and confidence. "We have much to do, Liorael. This is just the beginning." As Thor wandered into the habitat and laid down in front of the fire, Liorael noticed how tired he looked. His constant vigilance, roaming the Forbidden Forest to ensure no human intruders had entered, took a toll on him. She felt a surge of gratitude for his unwavering dedication.

Sanction approached Thor, gently patting his massive head. "You've done well, my friend," he said softly. "Rest now. We are safe for the moment." Liorael watched the interaction, feeling a deep sense of appreciation for both Sanction and Thor. Their efforts to protect the forest and her transformation filled her with a renewed sense of purpose.

As the flames danced in the hearth, the three of them—Sanction, Liorael, and Thor—found a moment of peace in the heart of the forest. The ancient ruins, the vibrant flora, and the enchanted creatures around them formed a sanctuary of magic and mystery, where Liorael's journey was just beginning.

Liorael looked at Sanction, And asked about something that had been bothering her since the first day they met."Sanction, what is it with the red and black moths, will I also have that ability?"Sanction turned to her, his eyes twinkling with understanding. "Ah, the red and black moths," he said, a hint of a smile on his lips. "They are a manifestation of the forest's ancient magic. They grant me the ability to traverse the forest swiftly and unseen, merging with its essence."

He paused, contemplating her question. "As for you, Liorael, your transformation is unique. The forest has its ways of bestowing gifts upon its chosen ones. While you might not have the exact same ability, you will develop powers that are uniquely yours. Powers that will be revealed to you as you grow stronger and more attuned to the forest."

Liorael nodded, feeling a mix of anticipation and wonder. "So, I might have abilities that are just as special?" "Indeed," Sanction replied. "The forest's magic is vast and varied. Trust in your journey, and you will uncover your own extraordinary abilities."Sanction smiled at Liorael's realization. "Exactly," he said, his tone filled with admiration.

"Your ability to blend into your surroundings is extraordinary. It's a gift from the forest that makes you unique and powerful in your own way. While I have my own set of abilities, like the red and black moths, your chameleon-like talent is something I could never possess."

He paused, letting his words sink in. "Every guardian of the forest has their own special connection and powers. Embrace your abilities, Liorael. They will guide and protect you in ways you can't yet imagine. The forest chose you for a reason, and it's revealing its magic to you because it trusts in your strength and potential."

Liorael felt a surge of confidence and curiosity. The forest's magic was vast, and her transformation was just the beginning of a journey filled with discovery and wonder. She wandered over to Thor who was already sound asleep and she cuddled up to him, As I watched I couldn't tell she was next to him her chameleon blended her perfectly to him making it look as its all him.

As dawn broke, an eerie stillness hung over the forest. The usual rustling of leaves and chirping of birds was conspicuously absent, replaced by an oppressive silence. Thor, usually a picture of calm, was pacing back and forth outside, his massive form tense and alert.

CHAPTER FIVE
DANGER IS NEAR

LIORAEL WOKE WITH A START, her instincts immediately sensing the disturbance. She glanced over at Sanction, who was already up, his eyes scanning the surroundings with a mix of concern and determination.

"What is it, Sanction?" she asked, her voice barely above a whisper, not wanting to break the fragile silence. Sanction shook his head, his expression grim. "Something is amiss. The forest is too quiet, and Thor's unease is a sign that danger might be near."

Liorael felt a shiver run down her spine. The forest, which had become her sanctuary, now felt like a place of impending doom. She stood up, her senses on high alert, ready to face whatever threat was lurking in the shadows.

"Stay close, Liorael," Sanction instructed, gripping his staff tightly. "We must be prepared for anything." Together, they stepped outside, their eyes scanning the misty landscape, ready to confront whatever had disturbed the peace of the Forbidden Forest.

The transformation of the forest around them was both unsettling and poignant. The once lively vines, now retreating underground, and the foliage collapsing into a dormant state painted a stark picture of the forest's distress. Sanction tightened his grip on his staff, his expression grim. "The forest is reacting to a threat," he said quietly. "Something has disturbed its balance."

Liorael felt a pang of fear and sadness as she watched the vibrant life of the forest retreat. "What do we do?" she asked, her voice trembling."Stay here Liorael, Thor protect" Liorael watched in awe as Sanction's body dissolved into a flurry of red and black moths, scattering in every direction. She felt a mix of fear and anticipation, knowing that whatever lay ahead was beyond her understanding but crucial for the forest's survival.

With Thor by her side, she took a deep breath, trying to steady her nerves. The massive wolf, sensing her anxiety, nudged her gently, his presence providing a comforting anchor. She crouched down, resting a hand on Thor's thick fur. "We'll stay here, just like Sanction said," she whispered, her voice firm despite the uncertainty swirling inside her. "We have to trust him."

The forest around them was eerily silent, the once vibrant foliage now dormant. Liorael felt a pang of sadness for the creatures and plants that had withdrawn, their magic stifled by the unknown threat. She knew she had to be strong, not just for herself, but for the entire forest.

As the minutes stretched into what felt like hours, Liorael's mind raced with questions and concerns. What was causing the disturbance? How would Sanction stop it? And most importantly, what role would she play in this unfolding crisis? With Thor's steady presence and her own determination, Liorael resolved to face whatever came next. She was part of this forest now, and she would protect it with everything she had.

The red and black moths traveled far and near till they saw the red flames bellowing up into black smoke, The flames engulfing everything in its path. Sanction's moths swirled around the devastating scene, witnessing the red flames licking hungrily at everything in their path. Black smoke billowed into the sky, choking the once vibrant forest with its dark embrace. The forest's pain was palpable, and Sanction knew they had to act quickly to stop the destruction.

The moths, carrying the urgency of the situation, scattered back towards the habitat, weaving through the foliage and shadows with haste. Sanction reformed his body, materializing before Liorael and Thor with a grave expression.

"Liorael, there is a fire," he said, his voice tense but resolute. "We must stop it before it consumes the entire forest." Liorael felt a surge of determination. The forest had given her so much, and now it needed her help. "What can I do?" she asked, ready to face the danger head-on. Sanction placed a hand on her shoulder. "Your connection to the forest, your ability to blend and communicate with it, will be crucial. We must harness the forest's magic to extinguish the flames and protect our home."

With Thor by their side, the three set off towards the heart of the inferno, ready to confront the fire and save the enchanted forest they called home. The sight of the raging flames and the forest's anguished cries fueled a fierce determination within Liorael. She couldn't stand by and watch her beloved home be consumed by fire.

Harnessing the magic that flowed through her veins, Liorael reached out with her senses, feeling the pain of the trees, the desperation of the creatures, and the life force of the forest itself. She whispered to the foliage, urging it to wake from its dormancy and rise to defend their shared home.

The forest responded to her call. Vines and roots surged from the ground, reaching toward the flames. Trees bent and twisted, creating barriers to slow the fire's advance. The air around them shimmered with magic as Liorael poured her energy into the land, guiding it to fight back.

Sanction, witnessing her growing power, added his own magic to the effort. Together, they created a formidable force against the inferno. Thor stood guard, his presence a reminder of the forest's strength and resilience.

As they battled the flames, Liorael's skin shifted colors, blending with the smoke and foliage, making her nearly invisible. She moved through the forest like a ghost, her actions swift and precise. She directed the water from hidden springs to douse the flames, and urged the creatures to safety.

Bit by bit, the relentless advance of the fire began to slow. The forest, with Liorael and Sanction at its helm, fought back with all its might. It was a grueling battle, but their combined strength and determination started to turn the tide. Liorael's connection to the forest deepened with every passing moment. She felt its gratitude and its hope, knowing that together, they could overcome this threat and restore balance to their home.

The fire was out, But Liorael felt sadness and still uneasy inside her. She looks at Sanction who was slumping down on the ground, His face showing signs of distress and worn out. Liorael's heart ached with the weight of what they had just endured. The fire might be out, but the scars it left behind were fresh and raw. The forest's cries of pain still echoed in her mind, and the smell of charred wood lingered in the air. She glanced over at Sanction, who was slumped on the ground, his face etched with exhaustion and distress. She hurried to his side, her heart pounding with worry.

"Sanction," she whispered, kneeling beside him. "Are you okay?" Sanction managed a weak smile, though his eyes betrayed the toll the battle had taken on him. "I'll be fine, Liorael," he said, his voice raspy. "The forest needed us, and we answered. But the fight has drained me."

CHAPTER SIX
SANCTION'S REVELATION

LIORAEL FELT A SURGE OF DETERMINATION. She had to be strong for both of them. Gently, she placed a hand on Sanction's shoulder, feeling the energy of the forest still pulsing through her. "We'll get through this," she said softly. "Together, we'll heal the forest and ourselves."

Thor, sensing the gravity of the moment, padded over and laid down beside them, his presence a comforting reminder of the strength and unity they shared. As the first light of dawn began to break through the trees, Liorael knew their journey was far from over. The forest needed time to heal, and so did they. But with Sanction and Thor by her side, she felt ready to face whatever challenges lay ahead.

Sanction sat quietly, feeling the weight of the forest's magic and the toll it had taken on him. He knew the time had come to reveal the truth to Liorael. With a heavy heart, he beckoned her to join him.

"Liorael," he began, his voice soft yet filled with resolve, "there is something I need to tell you. The forest's magic is ancient and powerful, but it comes with a price. My time as its guardian is coming to an end. "Liorael's eyes widened, her heart pounding.

"What do you mean, Sanction?" she asked, her voice trembling. "You're the guardian of the forest. I can't do this without you."

Sanction placed a gentle hand on her shoulder, his eyes filled with warmth and sadness. "You are stronger than you know, Liorael. The forest chose you because it sensed your potential and your strength. My role was to guide you, to prepare you for the day when you would take over as the forest's protector."

Tears welled up in Liorael's eyes. "But I'm not ready," she whispered. "I still have so much to learn." Sanction smiled softly. "You will learn, and you will grow. The forest's magic is within you, and it will guide you as it has guided me. I will always be a part of this forest, and a part of you. But the time has come for you to step into your destiny."

Liorael felt a mix of fear and determination. She knew that the path ahead would be challenging, but with Sanction's faith in her and the forest's magic coursing through her veins, she felt a glimmer of hope.

"Thank you, Sanction," she said, her voice steadying. "I will do my best to honor the forest and protect it as you have." Sanction nodded, his heart swelling with pride. "I know you will, Liorael. The forest is in good hands." Sanction with the help of Liorael and Thor they headed back to their habitat, once there they brought Sanction in and gently sat him in his chair.

Sanction settled into his worn-out chair. Thor, ever vigilant, lay down at his feet, eyes darting around as if sensing the gravity of the moment. Liorael, her heart heavy with the knowledge of what Sanction had just shared, knelt beside him.

The fire crackled softly, casting warm, flickering shadows on the walls. Sanction looked at Liorael, his eyes filled with a mixture of pride and sorrow. "You have done well, Liorael. The forest is healing, thanks to you." Liorael nodded, though her mind was racing with thoughts and questions. "I will do everything I can to protect the forest, Sanction. I promise."

Sanction smiled weakly. "I know you will, child. And remember, even when I am gone, the forest's magic will always be with you, guiding and supporting you."

As the night wore on, Liorael stayed by Sanction's side, drawing strength from his presence and the bond they had formed. She knew that the path ahead would be challenging, but with Thor at her side and the magic of the forest within her, she felt ready to face whatever the future held.

A week has passed and Liorael can see Sanction slowing down rapidly, his movements are becoming disorganized and confusing for him. Liorael watched with a heavy heart as Sanction's condition worsened. His once sure and steady movements had become slow and disoriented. The toll of their recent battle and the weight of his long-held secrets were taking a visible toll on him.

Each day, she could see his strength waning, and it filled her with a sense of urgency. She spent as much time as she could by his side, learning everything he was able to teach her, absorbing his knowledge and wisdom.

"Sanction," she said softly one morning, as she helped him sit comfortably in his chair. "I can see how much this is affecting you. Is there anything more you need to tell me? Anything that can help me understand my role better?"

Sanction looked at her with eyes that still held the spark of ancient wisdom, even as his body weakened. "Liorael, you have learned so much, and you have shown great strength and compassion. There is one last thing I need to share with you."

He took a deep breath, gathering his remaining energy. "The forest's magic is vast and eternal, but it needs a guardian to channel and protect it. When I am gone, that responsibility will fall to you. It is a great honor, but also a great burden. Trust in yourself and the bond you have with the forest. It will guide you, as it has guided me."

Liorael nodded, determination and sadness mixing within her. "I promise to protect the forest, Sanction. I will do my best to honor everything you have taught me." Sanction smiled faintly, his eyes closing as he leaned back. "I know you will, Liorael. You are ready."

The days that followed were filled with quiet moments, as Liorael prepared herself for the inevitable. The forest sensed the change as well, its magic subtly shifting in anticipation of its new guardian. Liorael knew that soon, she would have to take on the mantle of protector, and she steeled herself for the challenges ahead.

CHAPTER SEVEN
SANCTION PASSING THE STAFF

"LIORAEL HELP ME GO OUTSIDE PLEASE" Liorael helped Sanction outside and handed him his staff once they was clear of the habitat they shared. As they stepped outside, the early morning sun cast a gentle light over the forest, illuminating the vibrant foliage and the faint mist that still lingered. Sanction leaned heavily on his staff, drawing strength from the forest's magic that pulsed through it.

They walked slowly, Liorael supporting him with every step. She could feel the weight of what was to come, but she remained resolute. Sanction paused by an ancient tree, its massive trunk covered in intricate patterns of moss and vines.

"Liorael," he began, his voice filled with a quiet determination, "this is a place of great significance. It's where my journey began, and it's fitting that it's where I pass on my responsibilities to you."

He raised his staff, the air around them shimmering with magic. The tree seemed to respond, its leaves rustling softly as if acknowledging the moment. Sanction turned to Liorael, his eyes filled with pride and a hint of sorrow.

"You are ready, Liorael. The forest has chosen well. Trust in yourself, and in the magic that binds us all." Liorael felt a wave of emotion wash over her. She took a deep breath, standing tall. "I will honor you and the forest, Sanction. I will protect it with everything I have."

Sanction smiled, a serene expression on his face. "I know you will, child. The forest is in good hands." With that, he slowly handed his staff to Liorael, the weight of the ancient wood feeling both heavy and empowering in her hands. As she accepted it, she felt a surge of energy, the forest's magic flowing through her, intertwining with her own.

Sanction's time was ending, but Liorael's journey was just beginning. Together, they stood as guardians of the forest, ready to face whatever challenges lay ahead. As the forest creatures gathered, their eyes reflecting the ancient magic and witnessing the passing of the torch, the air buzzed with silent reverence. Liorael, with the staff firmly in her grasp, felt the weight of responsibility and the deep connection to every living being around her.

Thor, sitting tall and proud, epitomized the loyalty and strength that had been central to Sanction's life. His presence was a comforting constant in this pivotal moment. As the creatures bowed their heads in respect, the forest seemed to breathe a sigh of acceptance and continuity. Sanction, though weakened, smiled with pride and peace, knowing he had completed his role.

Liorael, surrounded by the ancient trees and the vibrant life of the forest, stood as the new guardian, ready to embrace her destiny and carry on the legacy of protecting this magical realm. In that somber moment, Liorael watched as Sanction's form dissolved into a swarm of red and black moths. His life force, once a guiding light, now scattered to every corner of the Forbidden Forest. It was a beautiful, yet heart-wrenching sight.

The forest creatures, sensing the significance of the event, bowed their heads in silent respect. Thor sat stoically, his eyes reflecting a profound understanding and sorrow. Liorael stood amidst the swirling moths, feeling the weight of her new role settling upon her shoulders.

As the moths dispersed, spreading Sanction's essence

throughout the forest, Liorael felt a surge of energy and determination. The forest's magic now flowed through her more intensely than ever before. She knew that Sanction's legacy lived on in her, and she would honor his memory by protecting and nurturing the forest as its new guardian.

The path ahead would be challenging, but Liorael was ready to embrace her destiny. With Thor by her side and the forest's magic within her, she felt a renewed sense of purpose and strength. Liorael enters the habitat that she shared with Sanction and watches Thor go over and sniff his old worn out chair and sits down on his hind legs and let out a loud howl.

The sound of Thor's mournful howl echoed through the habitat, a poignant tribute to Sanction. Liorael felt the weight of his absence, a void that seemed almost too vast to fill. She walked over to Thor, her heart heavy with sorrow and determination.

Kneeling beside him, she gently placed a hand on his fur, feeling the warmth and strength beneath her fingers. "We'll honor him by protecting this forest," she whispered, her voice filled with resolve. "Together, we'll carry on his legacy."

The fire crackled softly in the hearth, casting flickering shadows that seemed to dance with memories of Sanction's wisdom and guidance. The habitat, once a place of learning and comfort, now felt like a sacred space, filled with the echoes of the past and the promise of the future.

Liorael knew that the journey ahead would be challenging, but with Thor by her side and the magic of the forest flowing through her, she felt ready to embrace her destiny as the new guardian of the Forbidden Forest.

The days flowed into one another as Liorael continued to grow stronger, ever vigilant over the Forbidden Forest. Thor, her steadfast companion, roamed the forest with unwavering dedication, ensuring its safety.

Each time Liorael saw a red or black moth fluttering by, her heart ached with longing. The moths served as a bittersweet reminder of Sanction, her wise and gentle mentor. She often found herself whispering silent wishes, hoping to see him materialize before her eyes, offering guidance and comfort.

Despite the sadness, Liorael felt a deep sense of purpose. She knew that Sanction's spirit lived on through the forest's magic and within her. His teachings and his presence were woven into the very fabric of her being.

Her connection to the forest grew deeper with each passing day. She could sense the subtle shifts in the environment, hear the whispers of the trees, and feel the pulse of life all around her. Liorael embraced her role as the guardian, determined to honor Sanction's legacy and protect the magic that bound them all.

The forest, once again vibrant and alive, stood as a testament to their resilience. And though Sanction was gone, his spirit continued to guide her, a silent yet powerful force that would forever remain a part of her journey.

CHAPTER EIGHT
LIORAEL'S JOURNEY

IT WAS GETTING LATE in the season and turning cold outside, Liorael figured it was a good time to sweep up inside her habitat, as she was sweeping Thor's hair balls and moving things she sees it behind Sanctions worn out chair, It was his worn out hat. The memories came flooding back. The first day she met him and remembering his strong gentle voice.

The sight of Sanction's worn-out hat brought a flood of emotions for Liorael. As the cool air of the late season seeped into the habitat, the memories of that first day, his strong, gentle voice, and his wise teachings filled her heart. She gently picked up the hat, feeling the rough texture of its brim, and a tear slipped down her cheek.

Holding the hat close, she whispered, "I miss you, Sanction." The weight of her new responsibilities felt a bit lighter with this tangible connection to her mentor. Thor, sensing her emotions, padded over and nuzzled her gently.

Liorael took a deep breath, feeling a renewed sense of purpose. She knew that Sanction's spirit was with her, guiding her every step. The forest, with its vibrant magic and ancient wisdom, was now her charge, and she would protect it with all her heart.

The forest creatures watched silently from the shadows, their bright eyes reflecting the trust they had in their new guardian. Liorael felt their support, a reminder that she was never alone. She put on his hat and sat outside, with a tear rolling down her cheek, the vines sense her sorrow and slithered to her and tenderly hugged her.

The gentle embrace of the vines, sensing her sorrow, brought a quiet comfort to Liorael. Sitting there with Sanction's hat, she felt a connection to him and the forest that was deeper than words. The vines' tender hug reassured her that she was never alone in her grief or her duties.

The forest creatures, watching from a distance, seemed to understand the significance of the moment. Liorael took solace in the fact that she was part of something much larger, a living, breathing entity that cared for her as much as she cared for it.

As the tear rolled down her cheek, she felt a renewed sense of purpose and determination. The forest was her responsibility now, and she would protect it with everything she had. Sanction's spirit, the magic of the forest, and the loyalty of Thor were all with her, guiding her forward.

DIVINE ENTITIES

CHAPTER ONE
THE ECHOES OF SILENCE

AS THE SUN dipped below the horizon, casting long shadows over the rolling hills of the countryside, Jake found himself enjoying the solitude of the open road. That is, until his car started to sputter. A sudden jolt, followed by a cloud of smoke billowing out from under the hood, shattered the tranquility. Within moments, the once trusty vehicle became eerily silent, leaving Jake stranded in the middle of nowhere.

He stepped out, coughing from the acrid smoke, and surveyed his surroundings. To his left, a dirt path led into the woods. To his right, a faint silhouette of a building loomed in the fading light. Desperate for help, Jake decided to head towards the building, hoping to find a phone or someone who could assist.

As he was walking towards the foreboding building, with a turbulent, stormy sky and flashes of lightning in the background. The dark clouds swirl ominously, hinting at the chaos and conflict to come.

The wind picked up, and it started to rain. He hurried his pace to get to the building. As he was almost running in the rain, he looked up and saw flickers of yellow light on the third floor. His heart pounded in his chest, a mixture of fear and determination driving him forward. The shadows seemed to dance in the windows, adding an eerie glow to the dilapidated facade.

Reaching the front door, he hesitated for a moment, listening to the sound of the rain beating against the worn wood and metal he saw the main door was chained shut and a thick heavy rusty chain with two big rusty locks kept them from being opened. Taking a deep breath, he started banging on the doors and yelling hoping whoever was upstairs could hear him.

The sound of his fists pounding on the doors echoed through the building, mingling with the relentless patter of the rain. His voice, strained and desperate, filled the empty corridors. "Is anyone there? Please, let me in!" he shouted, his words almost drowned out by the storm.

For a few agonizing moments, there was no response. His heart raced, and he could feel the cold seeping into his bones. He looked up and there was a sign above the door but it was so rotten and unreadable. He skedaddled to the right of the building, stepping back enough to see up into the broken glass windows, He saw nothing.

The rain continued to pour, drenching him as he peered through the jagged shards of glass. The darkness inside the building seemed impenetrable, revealing no hint of life or movement. Frustration and desperation gnawed at him, but he refused to give up.

He moved further along the side of the building, searching for any other way in. His eyes scanned the walls, looking for a window that wasn't completely shattered or a door that might offer another entrance. All the windows had bars on them. He wondered if it was to keep someone in or keep others from entering, his mind was playing tricks on him and he tried not thinking bad thoughts.

He came to another half of the building and it was totally falling in and crumbled, this wasn't a way in and he turned around and headed back to the front of the building, and in doing so he stepped further away so he could see the third floor and again he saw them same eerie flashes of yellow light.

Determined not to give up, he took a deep breath and approached the front door again, this time with more resolve. He banged on the doors harder and shouted louder, hoping to catch the attention of whoever was inside. "Is anyone there? Please, let me in!" Again no response, not even a sound of life was heard and a chill ran up his spine.

He darted to the left side of the building where it was much darker. He fumbled for his flashlight in his jacket, and as he shone it on the side of the building, he noticed that one of the window bars was partially detached from the window frame.

His heart raced as he realized this might be his chance to get inside. He approached the window cautiously, the rain soaking through his clothes as he examined the gap. With a bit of effort, he managed to pry the bar further away, creating enough space for him to squeeze through. Taking a deep breath, he hoisted himself up and wriggled through the opening.

CHAPTER TWO
ENTERING THE FORBIDDEN BUILDING

HERE HE IS STRADDLING on the window sill and took his flashlight out and shone him what was ahead of him then to his right then to his left, he never thought about shining it on the floor in front of him and he put the flashlight back in his jacket and jumped down onto the floor, what was waiting for him was broken slimy slippery glass and once his shoes hit the glass and shot out from underneath him and he fell back and slammed his head against the window sill.

Just as quickly he got in quickly it was lights out for him as his body slumped down against the wall and floor and everything went dark and quiet. There he lay, unmoving, with the rain belting his body from the storm outside. A trickle of blood dripped down from behind his head, pooling against the wall.

Three white orbs floated around the hall, passing through the walls of the interior. The sound of a scream echoed throughout the empty floors. On each floor, different colored orbs froze, trying to figure out where the scream came from.

The orbs seemed to communicate silently, their movements synchronized as they floated towards the source of the sound. The white orbs, glowing softly, led the way, while the colored orbs followed, casting eerie hues on the walls as they moved.

As they approached the room where he lay, the orbs hesitated, their light flickering as if in contemplation. The white orbs hovered closer, illuminating his still form and the blood trickling from his head. The colored orbs circled around, their light casting strange patterns on the walls.

Suddenly, the white orbs began to pulse with a brighter light, as if they had made a decision. They floated down to his body, their light enveloping him in a soft glow. One of the bright white orbs materialized into a young girl child. Her spirit knelt down beside the man's body, and even though her hand could be seen going through his arm, she sensed his living essence and felt his pain.

The girl's ethereal form glowed softly, her eyes filled with a mix of sadness and compassion. She reached out, her fingers passing through his arm as if trying to offer comfort. The connection between them seemed to transcend the physical, a bond formed through the shared experience of suffering.

As she knelt there, the other orbs hovered nearby, their light casting an otherworldly glow on the scene. The girl's presence seemed to bring a sense of calm to the chaotic environment, her gentle spirit a beacon of hope in the darkness. The young spirit girl called out to the yellow orbs for help. The yellow orbs materialized into young teenagers and began to search each room, looking for something they could use to move him out of the harsh weather. After some time, they found a gurney and rolled it back to the young girl.

The blue orbs, now materializing into younger children—not as young as the white orbs and not as old as the teens—gathered their powers together. With a gentle, ethereal coordination, they lifted his body onto the gurney and carefully rolled it into an empty room, sheltered from the storm outside.

Once he was safely away from the weather, all the children materialized back into orbs and slowly drifted back to their respective floors, their task complete. However, the young spirit girl remained in her form, staying with him to watch over and protect him.

As the man lay on the gurney, the room filled with a soft, comforting glow from the girl's presence. Her light seemed to seep into his being, easing his pain and calming his restless mind. "You're safe now," she whispered, her voice like a soothing melody. "Rest and recover. There is much you need to know, and I will be here to guide you." Not knowing if he was able to hear her ghostly voice, the young spirit girl remained vigilant. She needed supplies to help him, so she turned to the two other white orbs that had stayed close. "We need some things to help him recover," she whispered. "If you can't find them here, ask the others to help."

The white orbs darted through walls, going from room to room, searching for what she needed. Despite their best efforts, they found nothing. Determined, they floated to the back of the building where a stairway was blocked with broken cement and wood. With a faint shimmer, they disappeared up to the next floor and then the floor above that.

As the girl watched them go, she stayed by the man's side, her glowing presence a source of warmth and comfort in the otherwise cold and foreboding room. She knelt beside him, gently touching his forehead, hoping to ease his pain with her ethereal touch.

Upstairs, the white orbs communicated with the other spirits, their lights flickering as they sought assistance. The colored orbs, understanding the urgency, joined in the search. Together, they scoured the building for anything that could aid in the man's recovery.

Meanwhile, the young girl hummed a soft, soothing lullaby, her voice barely a whisper. She hoped the gentle melody would reach the man, providing him some solace as he lay there unconscious. She could sense his spirit, fragile and flickering like a candle in the wind, and she was determined to keep it from extinguishing.

She looked up and there by the old rusty front doors stood a black figure, she knew who this was and she wasn't going to give him the chance to take this man's soul. It waited patiently and just stood there.

Minutes turned into what felt like hours as the orbs searched tirelessly. At last, they returned with a collection of items: an old, dusty blanket, a bottle of water they found in an abandoned first aid kit, and a few scraps of clean cloth. They brought these items to the girl, their lights pulsing with a sense of accomplishment.

Grateful for their help, the girl used the blanket to cover the man, shielding him from the cold. She gently dabbed at the wound on his head with the cloth, cleaning it as best as she could. The bottle of water, though small, would be enough to keep him hydrated until he woke up. In doing so the black figure faded away into the shadows. Knowing he has lost his chance to collect this soul.

The man stirred and tried to sit up, feeling a sharp pain in his head. He attempted to open his eyes slightly and caught a glimpse of the young spirit girl before falling back down and slipping into unconsciousness once again.

The young girl stayed by his side, her glowing presence a guardian against the encroaching darkness. She reached out and placed her hand gently on his forehead, sensing his pain and fatigue. The warmth of her touch seemed to soothe him, allowing him to rest more peacefully.

The room was silent except for the sound of the rain outside and the faint hum of the ancient devices around them. The young girl's spirit illuminated the space, providing a comforting light in the midst of the storm. She knew that she had to protect him from the forces that sought to claim his soul and unravel the secrets that connected them.

As she watched over him, she began to hum the same soft lullaby, hoping that its melody would reach him in his dreams and offer some solace. She could sense his strength, and she knew that he had a crucial role to play in uncovering the mysteries of the building.

Time passed slowly, each moment filled with a mixture of hope and anxiety. The young spirit girl remained steadfast, her resolve unwavering. She would do everything in her power to ensure that he recovered and found the answers he sought.

Today he regained his posture and was sitting up and looking around, he felt his head and felt a bandage was wrapped around his head, he sat there looking around there was nothing not a soul could be seen. The place was in ruins and trash everywhere, walls were caving in and doors were laying on the floor.

CHAPTER THREE
MEETING THE SPIRITS

HIS MEMORIES WERE HAZY, but he remembered the young spirit girl. The sense of their presence lingered, even though they were nowhere to be seen now. He felt a strange mix of gratitude and determination.

He knew he had to find out more about this place and the spirit that had helped him. He got to his feet, still feeling a bit unsteady, and began to explore the room. As he moved through the debris, he spotted a faded photograph lying among the rubble. He picked it up and saw a picture of a family, their faces smiling despite the wear and tear on the photo. It gave him a glimpse into the past of this dilapidated building and the lives that had once been here.

Determined to uncover more, he made his way out of the room and into the hallway. The building's silence was almost deafening, broken only by the occasional creak and groan of the structure. He needed to find clues about the building's history and the secrets it held.

He headed to the big doors and noticed that this was a station, seeing file cabinets laying on their sides and some where open and old torn files scattered about, He picked up a file or two and saw it written admit patient number 1120, So this must been a hospital he said to himself.

He flipped through the pages of the file, his curiosity piqued. The documents contained various medical records, but they were mostly illegible due to age and damage. Nonetheless, the discovery confirmed his suspicion about the building's past.

As he continued to search the area, he found more clues about the hospital's history. Torn charts, faded photographs, and handwritten notes littered the floor. The stories of countless patients seemed to echo through the empty halls, their presence lingering in the shadows.

In the back part of the building there was little flicker of white light, he didn't notice them during his search of this level. His attention was drawn to a particularly old and worn journal lying partially hidden under a pile of debris. He picked it up and carefully opened it. The handwriting was difficult to read, but it seemed to be the personal notes of a doctor who had once worked there.

CHAPTER FOUR
JOURNAL ENTRY - DATE UNKNOWN

PATIENT #1120 has exhibited symptoms that none of the staff can explain. Despite our best efforts, the condition worsens daily. There is a growing sense of unease among the staff,I couldn't read much till I came to the end and it mentioned that they lost another young soul.

The weight of the realization hit him hard. This place, once a children's hospital, had seen so much suffering and loss. The thought of all the young lives that had ended here was overwhelming. He sat down on the floor, his head throbbing with pain and sorrow.

As he tried to process the information, the young spirit girl appeared beside him, her presence a comforting glow in the midst of his turmoil. She knelt down and placed a gentle hand on his shoulder, her touch soothing his aching head.

CHAPTER FIVE
SPIRITS WERE AT PEACE

"YOU'VE DISCOVERED THE TRUTH," she said softly. "This place was once a haven for children, but it became a place of sorrow and loss. Many young souls were lost here, and their spirits still linger, unable to find peace."

He looked up at her, his eyes filled with sadness. "Why are you still here?" he asked, his voice barely above a whisper. "We are bound to this place," she replied. "Our spirits cannot move on “For we are called Potter children.”

“Potter children?” I don’t understand what you mean? She stood up and looked behind her. One by one, the other orbs began to glow brighter and materialize into the forms of children of various ages. The room filled with their ethereal presence, each child's face reflecting a mix of innocence and anguish.

"As you see," she said softly, "we are bound here because our bodies were never claimed. Nobody missed us, nobody cared to come and give us a proper burial. We are nobodies."

Tears flooded his eyes as he listened to her words, the pain in his heart unbearable. The weight of their stories, the lives unlived and forgotten, crushed him with a sense of profound sorrow. These children, who should have been cherished and loved, were instead left behind, their spirits trapped in an eternal limbo.

He knelt down, his voice choked with emotion. "You are not nobodies," he said, his tears mingling with the dust on the floor. "You are important. I will remember you, and I will do everything I can to help you find peace."

The young spirit girl knelt beside him, her hand reaching out to touch his cheek. Though her fingers passed through him, he felt a warmth that soothed his aching heart. "Thank you," she whispered. "Your kindness means more than you can imagine."

Determined to honor the children and bring them the peace they deserved, he stood up, wiping away his tears. The journey ahead would be difficult, but with the spirits by his side, he felt a renewed sense of purpose.

There was a rumble towards the back of the building and a cloud of dust was pushed forward, blinding him. The children returned to their orb forms and disappeared. She stayed with him and told him something very important.

"Once this building collapses, our orbs will not be able to light, and we will be forced to wait out eternally, not knowing what to do. We just wait. It's what happened to the adult wing that is no longer standing."

"You mean there are adult orbs that used to be there as well and are now in limbo?" he asked, trying to grasp the gravity of the situation.

The young spirit girl nodded solemnly. "Yes, there were many adults whose spirits were also trapped here when the building collapsed. Without their orbs to guide them, they are lost in a state of eternal limbo, unable to find peace or move on."

His heart ached at the thought of countless souls, both young and old, trapped in an endless cycle of waiting and longing. He realized that time was of the essence. The building's instability meant that if it collapsed further, the remaining spirits would be condemned to the same fate.

Determined to prevent this, he stood up with renewed purpose. "I will do everything I can to help you and the others find peace," he vowed. “But I need to understand more about what happened here and how I can help.”

The young spirit girl looked at him with gratitude and hope. “Thank you,” she said softly. “There is a way. You must find the records and discover our names. Then, you need to find a priest to come here and bless this ground. But the biggest task is to find the Potter's Graveyard and our ashes, so we can be freed from here.”

He nodded, feeling the weight of the responsibility she had placed on his shoulders. "I'll do everything I can," he promised. "Where do I start?"

The girl gestured towards the darkened hallway. "Begin with the records in the main office. They should hold the information you need to find our names. Once you have them, you'll need to visit the Potter's Graveyard. It's a place where those who were forgotten were laid to rest. Our ashes must be there."

Taking a deep breath, he prepared himself for the task ahead. The journey would be difficult, but he was determined to see it through. He started down the hallway, the girl's spirit beside him, her presence a comforting reminder that he was not alone.

“I know this must sound weird to you, but I feel a positive connection with you. And since we are looking for names, what is your name?” he asked softly, feeling a strange sense of warmth despite the chilling atmosphere.

The young spirit girl looked at him, her eyes filled with a gentle glow. Even though they couldn't physically feel each other, she placed her hand in his and smiled. "My name is Isabella," she said softly.

The name carried a certain weight and tenderness, as if uttering it connected him more deeply to her and the many lost souls she represented. “Isabella,” he repeated, committing it to memory with a sense of respect and care.

“Thank you for sharing your name with me, Isabella,” he said, his voice filled with empathy. “I promise I will do everything I can to help you and the other children find peace.”

Isabella nodded, her spirit glowing brighter with renewed hope. "Let's start with the records in the main office," she said. "We need to find our names to begin the journey to the Potter's Graveyard." As he went through the files, he discovered that most of the remaining records were for the Potter children. It seemed that no one had needed these files, and luckily, they hadn't been destroyed. He carefully collected all the names, feeling the weight of each one as he read it.

With the list of names in hand, he and Isabella returned to the spot where he had slept. One by one, he called out each name. As he did, an orb would appear and materialize into a child. The room filled with the glowing forms of the children, their faces reflecting a mix of hope and sadness.

As each child materialized, they looked at him with a mixture of curiosity and gratitude. He felt a deep sense of responsibility and determination to help them find peace.

"Thank you for remembering us," one of the children said softly. "We've been waiting for so long."

"I will find the Potter's Graveyard," he promised. "And I will find a priest to bless this place. You will all be freed."

The children's spirits seemed to brighten at his words, their hope renewed. With the names in hand and the spirits gathered around him, he knew that the next steps would be crucial in their journey to peace.

The spirits watched him climb back out of the window he had entered many days ago. The orbs floated up to the third level, observing as he made his way to his car. As he walked, he remembered the events that had unfolded inside the building. He whispered a prayer, hoping for the souls to find peace.

Reaching his car, he got in and turned the key in the ignition. To his relief, the engine roared to life without any of the previous issues—no banging, no smoking—everything seemed to be working fine. It felt like a small blessing, a sign that he was on the right path.

CHAPTER SIX
"ISABELLA"

WITH THE NAMES of the Potter children safely in his pocket, he knew what he needed to do next. He drove away from the old hospital, determined to find the Potter's Graveyard and a priest who could bless the grounds. He was filled with a sense of purpose and hope, ready to uncover the final pieces of the puzzle and help the spirits find their peace.

As time passed, he finally located the Potter's Graveyard. In the basement of the caretaker's office, he found the ashes of all the children whose names he had discovered. With great care and reverence, he gathered each one and placed them tenderly in his trunk. The one labeled "Isabella" he put in a box lined with silk, setting it beside him in the passenger seat.

Now came the daunting task of finding a priest who would understand his story and not dismiss him as crazy. He knew this would be a challenge, but he was determined to see it through for the sake of the children.

Driving away from the graveyard, he felt a mix of hope and apprehension. He began his search for a priest, visiting churches and explaining his findings. With each conversation, he hoped to find someone who would listen and believe in the urgency of his mission.

The priest, Father Michael, was a compassionate man who had seen and heard many strange things in his lifetime. He could sense the sincerity and desperation in the man's words.

"I believe you," Father Michael said, his eyes filled with understanding. "And I will help you. Let's go to the hospital and bless the grounds, and we'll pray for the souls of these children."

With a sense of relief and gratitude, he and Father Michael set off together, returning to the old hospital. The journey was filled with a renewed sense of purpose. They arrived at the building, and Father Michael began the blessing, reciting prayers and sprinkling holy water around the premises.

With each blessing and a name was said out loud and their urn was open and spread freely into the wind The priest witnessed something he never seen before, A orb would be present and materialized into a child and we watch each child head for the heavens.

It was Isabella time but I had a surprise for her, during all this time she was standing there from inside the building looking at us and watched her companions being called home. I climbed inside the building and the priest was at the window waiting and was watching me for a sign.

Isabella I have a special surprise for you, I got down on my knees in front of her spirit form and it looked like I was holding her hands in mine, "if it wasn't for your compassion and treatment I could have died, During this time with you I think you deserve this more than anything Isabella I made you part of my family you are somebody you have a full name and a loving family waiting for you"

Even though she was a ghost spirit she was tearing up and so was I. Your ashes I will be bringing to our family plot and you will have a decent place to rest and I wanted to tell you that I was able to make this legal, You are legally my step daughter.

I nodded at the priest as he was saying the rites, and Isabella gave me a hug. Two bright orange orbs descended from heaven, materializing behind Isabella. There stood my holy grandparents from heaven. Since I made Isabella my stepdaughter, they had come down to bring her home.

Isabella's face lit up with a mixture of surprise and joy. She turned to see the two radiant figures who had come to guide her. With tears in her eyes, she looked back at me, her gratitude and love shining brighter than ever.

"Thank you," she whispered, her voice filled with emotion. "You have given me a family and a place to belong. I will never forget you."

With one final hug, Isabella's spirit began to merge with the orange orbs, her form glowing brighter as she prepared to ascend. My grandparents smiled warmly, their presence a comforting assurance that Isabella would be well taken care of in the afterlife.

As they began their journey back to heaven, a sense of peace and fulfillment washed over me. The spirits of the children were finally free, and Isabella had found her way home. The old building, once a place of sorrow, now stood as a silent testament to the power of love and compassion.

The priest and I stood in reverent silence, watching as the orbs disappeared into the sky. The journey had been long and filled with challenges, but the spirits were at peace, and so was I.

Father Michael took out his Bible and began reading verses I didn't recognize. He blessed the area where the adult wing had collapsed. As he finished, the ground shook, and parts of the collapsed building shifted. Suddenly, many more orbs gathered, glowing brightly, and they too ascended to the heavens.

The sight was awe-inspiring. The spirits of the adults, who had been trapped in limbo for so long, were finally finding peace. Father Michael and I watched in reverent silence as the orbs floated upwards, joining the children in their journey to the afterlife. The air seemed to hum with a sense of closure and release.

With the spirits freed and the building now quiet, the oppressive atmosphere that once hung over the place lifted. The sense of fulfillment was overwhelming, knowing that both the children and adults had found their way home.

Father Michael placed a comforting hand on my shoulder. "You've done a great thing here," he said. "You've given these souls the peace they've been waiting for."

I nodded, feeling a mixture of relief and gratitude. The journey had been arduous, but every step had been worth it. The spirits were finally at rest, and I knew that Isabella and all the others were now in a place where they were loved and remembered.

The next day I contacted the funeral home and they prepared everything for me and I brought Isabella urn, her ashes and with Father Michael we had a service and Isabella was laid to rest between my grandparents graves. I got down on my knees and laid a red rose down on top of Isabella's urn and I swear I could faintly see my grandparents' outlines standing there with Isabella between them. Thank you Isabella for being there for me and I'm proud to accept you into our family. God Bless You and we will see each other someday.

ALSO BY KENNETH HAINES

A TALE OF ESCAPE

A group of Earthlings, including a young woman named Elara, is abducted by an invisible alien ship to become part of a cosmic exhibition. Facing the reality of being observed by an alien audience, they form a bond and ignite a longing for freedom. Together, they plot their escape, daring to dream of returning to their lives on Earth. As they navigate their captivity and fight for autonomy, they are tested but remain unbroken, driven by the hope of weaving their experiences back into humanity's story.

WHISPERS IN THE SAND

Amidst the whispers of the sand and the caress of the Autumn sea, a tale of survival unfolds on the shores of a forsaken island. Here, young Selene and her father carve out an existence, relying on the embrace of nature and each other. Their bond, once threatened by tragedy, burgeons under the trials they face in this barren refuge. But when the island yields an unexpected reunion, the fabric of their family is woven together once more, painting a poignant portrait of hope and resilience. In the cool embrace of a late afternoon's breeze, Selene's heart finds solace, and together, they etch a new beginning upon their souls—an indelible whisper in the fabric of time.

In the oppressive kingdom of Eldaf, where elves endure human cruelty, a desperate elf mother and her child find an unexpected ally in a compassionate human. Together, they embark on a perilous escape through secret paths and natural sanctuaries, aided by the whispers of the forest's denizens. Their journey leads them to an abandoned, tranquil cottage, where they begin a new life of resilience and love. United by courage and kinship, their bond transcends blood, offering hope and peace amidst the shadows of their past.

ECHOES OF LAUGHTER, ECHOES OF FEAR

In an abandoned amusement park reclaimed by nature, five young explorersâ€"three girls and two boysâ€"embark on an adventure filled with mystery and spectral intrigue. Amid peeling paint and rusting rides, they delve into the park's hidden sorrows, blending nostalgia with a sense of foreboding. As they confront both the park's secrets and their own fears, their journey becomes a test of courage, friendship, and the human spirit. In this eerie yet captivating odyssey, the line between joy and darkness blurs, leaving them to discover whether their bonds can light the way through the park's enigmatic shadows.

SEA OF SHADOWS

Stranded on a solitary island, young Helene navigates a journey of survival and self-discovery, guided by the wisdom of her late father and the lessons of the untamed wilderness. Amid the island's deceptive tranquility, she transforms grief into resilience, building a sanctuary from remnants of the past and forging a future shaped by love and fortitude. Through hardship, Helene finds strength in enduring connections, her father's presence ever a guiding light. Her odyssey is one of emotional catharsis and renewal, where each dawn heralds the triumph of hope and the radiance of new beginnings.

www.ingramcontent.com/pod-product-compliance
Lightning Source LLC
LaVergne TN
LVHW010504160826
845677LV00012B/2651

* 9 7 9 8 8 9 6 9 1 3 3 8 2 *